GRANDPA'S GOALSCARERS

TONY LEE and
BEN SCRUTON

EDGE
FRANKLIN WATTS

LONDON·SYDNEY

Franklin Watts
First published in Great Britain in 2018 by The Watts Publishing Group

Text copyright © Tony Lee 2018
Illustration copyright © Ben Scruton 2018

Illustrator: Ben Scruton
Design Manager: Peter Scoulding
Cover Designer: Cathryn Gilbert
Production Manager: Robert Dale
Series Consultant: Paul Register
Executive Editor: Adrian Cole

HB ISBN 978 1 4451 5694 1
PB ISBN 978 1 4451 5695 8
Library ebook ISBN 978 1 4451 5696 5

Printed in China.

Franklin Watts
An imprint of
Hachette Children's Group
Part of The Watts Publishing Group
Carmelite House
50 Victoria Embankment
London EC4Y 0DZ

An Hachette UK Company
www.hachette.co.uk

www.franklinwatts.co.uk

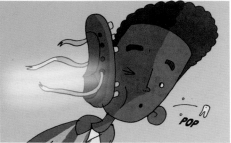

14